The Most Perfect Spot

By Diane Goode

HarperCollins*Publishers*

The Most Perfect Spot
Copyright © 2006 by Diane Goode
Manufactured in China. All rights reserved. No part
of this book may be used or reproduced in any manner
whatsoever without written permission except in the case of brief
quotations embodied in critical articles and reviews. For information
address HarperCollins Children's Books, a division of HarperCollins
Publishers, 1350 Avenue of the Americas, New York, NY 10019 •
www.harperchildrens.com
Library of Congress Cataloging-in-Publication Data • Goode, Diane.
The most perfect spot / by Diane Goode. — 1st ed. •   p.   cm.
Summary: Jack tries to have a perfect picnic with his mother, but things
do not turn out as they expected. • ISBN-10: 0-06-072697-0 — ISBN-
10: 0-06-072698-9 (lib. bdg.) • ISBN-13: 978-0-06-072697-3 —
ISBN-13: 978-0-06-072698-0 (lib. bdg.) • [1. Picnicking—Fiction.
2. Mothers and sons—Fiction.] I. Title. • PZ7.G604Mos
2006   [E]—dc22 • 2004030058   CIP   AC • Design
by Stephanie Bart-Horvath • 1 2 3 4 5 6 7
8 9 10 ❖ First Edition

For Peter,
the most perfect son
Love, Mom

One sunny morning,

Jack made his mama breakfast in bed,
and a card that said,

"I know the most perfect spot for a picnic."

So Mama put on her very best hat,
and they set off for Prospect Park.

The sky was clear and blue.
It was the perfect day for a picnic.

They walked around the corner
and through the big park gate.

They followed a wooded path until
they came to the lake. The water was calm.

It seemed like the most perfect spot.
So Jack helped his mama into a boat.

BUT...
...suddenly,

who knows why,

a flock of ducks flapped their wings

and cried, *"Quack, quack! Quack, quack!"*

The noise startled Mama. *Splash!*
She fell into the lake.
Splash! Jack fell in too.

"Brrrr. . . ." Jack and Mama were wet and cold,
so they went to dry off in the sun.
It seemed like the most perfect spot.

BUT . . .

. . . . suddenly,

who knows why,

five riders on horseback came galloping by.

Clippety-clop! Clippety-clop! Splat!

Split, splat. The horses kicked up the mud.
It got all over Mama and Jack.

So Jack took his mama to the carousel,
where they'd be safe from ducks and horses.
It seemed like the most perfect spot.

BUT . . .
. . . suddenly,

who knows why,

the carousel went around—

Whoosh, whoosh! Whoooooosh!—very, very fast.

Wooooo. . . . The ride made Mama dizzy,
and she could not find her hat.

There were gray clouds in the sky.
Jack and Mama were too tired and
too hungry to look for Mama's hat,

so they plopped down in a meadow.

It was noisy—"*Yakety-yak-yak*"—and before

they could eat, it began to rain, *pitter-patter-pitter, pat . . .*

. . . and suddenly, who knows why, a pack of dogs ran past,

barking, *"Arf, arf! Woof, woof!"* And then it began to pour!

"This park does NOT have the most perfect
spot for a picnic!" Jack said. So he took his mama by the
hand and they ran through a park gate.

They

did

not

look

back!

They ran around the corner, *splish-splash, squish.*
They ran through the wet streets . . .

. . . and all the way up the stairs.

Back home to the best picnic spot.

Just Mama and Jack . . .

. . . and a dog they named Spot,

the most perfect Spot!